Release the CHICKENS!

Release the Chickens!
Copyright © 2020 Travis M. Blair
Text: Travis M. Blair
Illustration: Paige Connelly

Editor: Amy Waeschle

ISBN: 978-1-7349272-1-4

Published by Zarfling Platoon
info@zarfling.com
zarfling.com

FROM THE
HEARTY
EGGS
FARM
COLLECTION

Release the CHiCKENS!

WRITTEN BY
TRAVIS M. BLAIR

ILLUSTRATED BY
PAIGE CONNELLY

On an early fall morning at Hearty Eggs Farm,
many animals are getting ready for a day's work.

There are one hundred chatting chickens,

a sewing goat named Zeus,

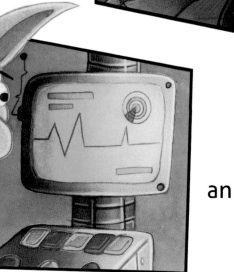

an inventor pig named Bruce,

a guard dog
named Fluke,

and a delivery cow
named Ethel.
All animals have jobs
at the farm.

This farm is a bit different than other farms, however.
Thanks to Lucy the chicken, Hearty Eggs Farm sells a lot of eggs.

The secret about the farm is it sells eggs to customers near and very, very far.

Bruce is creative. He accidentally invented a portal to another land! It's as if you could walk through an open door to a new place. Some visitors arrived, looking to buy a lot of eggs.

Bruce made a new and improved portal. It looks like a giant horseshoe.

Here comes Ethel, pulling the cart for egg deliveries! Lucy is also enjoying a ride. Ethel does not say much. She does her job, no questions asked.

Look, there are the customers! These are gnomes, and they like to keep all of their eggs in one basket.

The gnomes take the eggs to their village, and the eggs get cooked into omelets large enough to feed their village. They return the empty basket to Ethel.

What's this? There appears to be a goblin, spying from behind a bush inside the village! There are some others. What are they planning to do?

Later in the evening, a noise is heard from inside the barn. It is coming from the empty basket the gnomes had returned earlier. It's a goblin! He has been hiding inside!

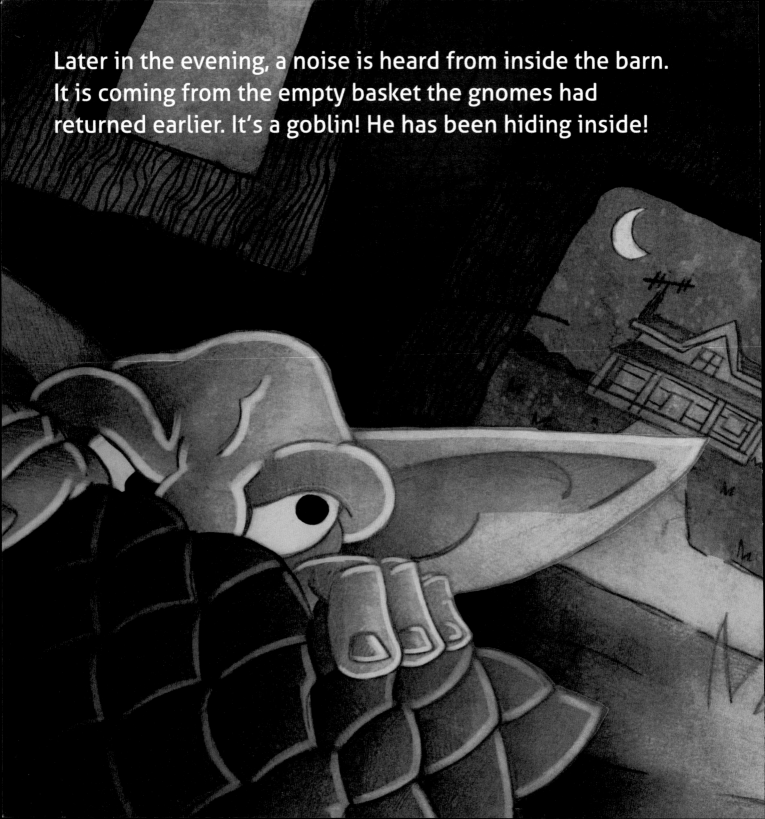

The sneaky goblin turns on the portal. Lights can be seen glowing from within the barn. Under the cover of darkness, several other sneaky goblins rush from the gnome village, into the portal, and appear at the farm.

"Help! Help!" yells Fluke the guard dog.
"The chickens have been taken!"

Fluke reports to his boss, the farmer.
"Goblins were seen fleeing the farm
with dozens of sleeping chickens!"

Fluke sees a gnome. "I just came from the village. Your portal is still open! Goblins took your chickens!"

Farmer Hank, still in his pajamas, is shocked. "Goblins took our chickens? Goblins took our chickens!"

Bruce runs to the barn. The portal is on.
The gnome shows his village on the other side.

Ethel speaks up. "I carry baskets full of eggs. I also carry a lot of empty baskets. I did not notice that an empty basket was hiding someone inside. It is my fault the chickens were taken."

Farmer Hank, now drinking some coffee, is awake. "This is not your fault Ethel! We had no idea someone wanted our eggs bad enough to steal our hens. You do your job every day without--"

But his nice words were not heard. Ethel raced past him, with the cart in tow. It looks like others are going with her!

Ethel gallops into the new land to rescue the chickens. The helpful gnome joins them.

Ethel gets directions from him. "Go left! I think I know where they went!"

The group hears a harsh whisper from behind a nearby tree. "Psst...quick, hide here!"

"Me name's Lux. I know why you here. Those chickens of you, yeah?" The goblin shows them a knitted hat, left by one of the hens.

"Stealing is wrong. If they goblins want eggs, they need to pay for 'em. I help you to get chickens of you while goblins are sleep."
Lux jumps on Zeus.

They sneak past the sleeping goblins and find the cages holding the chickens. Zeus finds Lucy! "We found your hat!" whispers Zeus.

Ethel gallops back to the portal, pulling a crowded cart.

The following morning, the sneaky goblins wake and wonder. "Where goes chickens?" one yells. "Those all left us!" yells another.

Lux teaches the other goblins how to pay for what they want.

The residents of Hearty Eggs Farm prepare for their next delivery. They recognize the hard work Ethel does for the farm, by adding her own basket to the cart.

Ethel the cow delivers to her first customer.

Made in the USA
Middletown, DE
26 September 2021